ELLEN ROSS
PRIVATE
DETECTIVE

Written by Adrian Robert

Illustrated by T.R. Garcia

Troll Associates

Library of Congress Cataloging in Publication Data

Robert, Adrian.
 Ellen Ross, private detective.

 Summary: When Terry doesn't allow Ellen to play police
detective with him, Ellen becomes a private detective
on her own. Then Terry finds he really does need her
help on an important case.
 1. Children's stories, American. [1. Mystery and
detective stories] I. Garcia, T.R., ill. II. Title.
PZ7.R5385El   1985   [E]   84-8744
 ISBN 0-8167-0414-7 (lib. bdg.)
 ISBN 0-8167-0415-5 (pbk.)

ELLEN ROSS PRIVATE DETECTIVE

It all started with Terry's birthday party.
Terry lives next door. He had a great party.
There were three-decker sandwiches. There
was an ice-cream cake and lots of balloons.

We played some really good games. Only
one lamp got broken. Dinky Bragg pinned
the tail on Sarah Greening, and she cried.
And Terry got lots of great presents.

Terry's grandfather the policeman sent him a Police Detective Kit. It was in a shiny black box with a handle. Inside were a water pistol and some false mustaches. There were handcuffs. There was a notebook and a pen filled with invisible ink. There was a fingerprint set. There was a magnifying glass. There was even a badge and a wallet with an I. D. card.

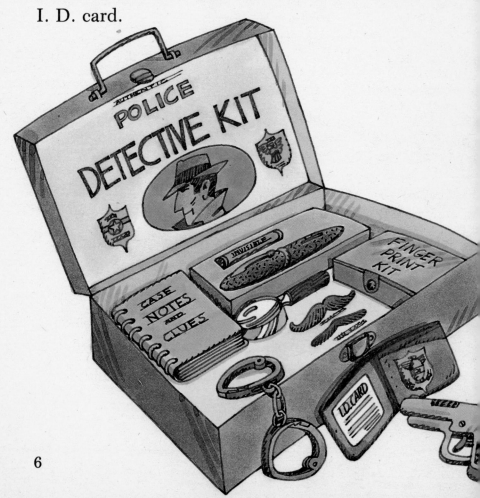

"What's that?" Sarah asked.

"An identification card," said Terry.
"It shows who I am."

The card even had Terry's picture pasted
on it. Terry printed his name on it carefully:
TERRY SANDERS, DETECTIVE CAPTAIN.

Terry pinned on the badge. He puffed out
his chest. He was pleased.

We didn't play detectives then. It was time to go home. Next morning at breakfast, Dad said, "Why is Terry crawling under our porch, and why is he wearing a false mustache?"

I jumped up. Mom said, "Finish your
breakfast, young lady!" I knew better than to
argue. I ate my cereal fast. Then I ran
outside.

All I could see were Terry's sneakers and part of his jeans. They were sticking out from under the porch steps. I called, "Terry!" He didn't answer. So I yelled, "Captain Sanders!" as loudly as I could.

Terry crawled out. He was wearing a black mustache, and he was angry. "Shhhhhh!" he hissed. He looked over his shoulder. Then he leaned forward and whispered, "I'm on a case. I'm looking for a dangerous criminal."

"I'll help," I said. "I'll be a detective, too."

Terry snorted. "Huh! Girls can't be detectives!"

Terry is six weeks older than I am. That means he thinks he knows more. It was my turn to get angry.

"That's all you know!" I said. "My cousin
Mary is a detective. I'm going to be a
detective just like her."

Terry and I glared at each other. We
always played together on Saturday
mornings. "Tell you what," Terry said.
"You can be my assistant. You can follow me
around and do things for me."

I was too mad to answer. So I just ran up the steps. At the door, I turned around and yelled, "Anyway, you're a dumb detective! There aren't any dangerous criminals on our street!"

Terry and I didn't play together once all
weekend. I was pretty lonely. Mom told me
to think about what good friends Terry and I
were. She told me maybe I was being silly.

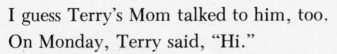

I guess Terry's Mom talked to him, too.
On Monday, Terry said, "Hi."

I said, "Hi."

He said, "I'm going to the empty lot out
back to look for pussy willows. Want to
come?"

I said, "Sure."

The empty lot was swampy and squishy.
We found pussy willows and almost caught a
frog. But we didn't talk about being
detectives.

After that, I still played with Terry.
But sometimes I'd see him go out alone.
He'd carry his case and wear a mustache and
his dad's old raincoat. And I'd get mad.

When my birthday came, I had a nice
party of my own. We went to the movies
and came back home for ice cream and cake.
I got lots of presents. I even got a Doctor Kit.
But I didn't get a Detective Kit.

The next day my cousin Mary came to
visit. I hadn't seen her since I was little.
She didn't look a bit like a real detective!
She had no false beard or magnifying glass.
She didn't even wear a raincoat.

"What's the matter, Ellen?" Mary said with a laugh. "Don't you believe I'm a detective?"

"I do," I said. "But my friend doesn't." I told her all about Terry. Mary shook her head.

"Terry's wrong. There are lots of women police detectives—and women private detectives, like me. Why don't you be a private detective, Ellen?"

I thought that was a great idea. Then I had an even better idea. Private Detective Ellen Ross was going to solve a case that Police Detective Terry Sanders couldn't solve.

Cousin Mary was terrific. She gave me my own magnifying glass. She made me an I. D. card that looked like hers. She showed me how to make invisible ink. "I'll write you letters with it," I told her.

"You can write me all about how you
solve your first case," said Mary.

I'll write how I solved the case that
baffled Terry Sanders, I thought.

After Mary left, I started watching for clues. It was hard to do that without Terry knowing. It was hard to find a case Terry couldn't solve. In fact, I couldn't find any case at all.

I spent every weekend looking for a case to solve. But during the week I had to think about school. We were studying the Grand Canyon. Dinky Bragg brought in color photos from his vacation to show the class.

"What makes the rocks all different colors?" Sarah Greening asked. So our teacher told us about the minerals in the rocks.

"There can be many different colors inside rocks," he said. "There can be purple and pink and blue and even green."

Terry put his hand up. "My mom has a ring made out of a green rock," he said.

"Huh!" said Dinky. "I don't believe that. There are no green rocks!"

Terry's face grew red. He didn't say anything. But the next day when we talked about the Grand Canyon he stuck his hand up again. On his finger was a gold ring. The stone in it looked like a slice of rock. And it was green!

"What a beautiful ring," our teacher said. We passed it around carefully. Then Terry put it back on his finger. "That way I won't lose it," he said.

When school got out, I went over to Terry. "How did you get your mom to let you bring that ring to school?" I asked.

Terry looked over his shoulder. He lowered his voice. "*Shh,*" he said. "I didn't ask. I just borrowed it. I'll put it back when I get home. Don't worry. Detective Sanders is on guard." He jammed his hands into the pockets of his raincoat like a TV detective.

We started walking home. Dinky and some other kids were playing kickball at the playground. "Come and play," they called.

Terry took off his raincoat. We left our books with the other kids' books. We played till we all were tired.

"Time to go home," I said.

"Me, too," said Terry. "Gee, my mom will be mad." Terry was a mess. He had a skinned knee and skinned knuckles. There were grass stains on his shirt. "I'll put my raincoat on," he said. "Then the dirt won't show so much."

We started home. "Maybe you can wash the dirt off," I said, "before anybody sees it."

"Maybe I can keep my hands in my pockets," Terry said. "So my knuckles won't show. I'll have to take them out for dinner, though." He took his hands out. Then he froze.

"What's the matter?" I asked. Then I looked and knew.

The green ring was gone.

"You must have dropped it on the playground," I said.

"Oh, no," Terry said. "What'll I do? We've got to go back and look."

"I thought the great detective didn't need help on his cases," I said.

Terry turned red. He said, "I need help now. My mom has a real temper. Come on, Ellen. I'll let you be a detective after all."

"I already am a detective," I said. "I'm a private detective, like my cousin Mary."

Terry swallowed hard. He took a deep breath and said, "Then can I hire you to work with me on this case?"

"All right," I said. "We'd better get back to the playground."

We looked all over the field where we had played. Some other kids were there, and they helped, too. We got down on our knees and crawled in the grass. There was no gold ring anywhere.

"Somebody must have found it," one of the kids said. "Too bad, Terry. You'd better go home."

Terry didn't want to go home. He didn't have to tell me, but I knew. He dug his hands into his raincoat pockets and tried to look tough.

We walked home without a word. I felt bad for Terry. And I felt bad for me. My first case—and I hadn't come up with a single clue.

I tried to think about when we'd last seen the ring. I thought about the ring going around in class. Then Terry put it back on his finger. I could see Terry coming out of school, digging his hands into his pockets.

I stopped walking. "Give me your coat,"
I said.

Terry looked at me. He started to say no. Then he changed his mind and took off the raincoat. I put my hands in the pockets and felt around.

No ring was there.

I almost couldn't believe the ring wasn't there. I felt around again. There was no ring in either pocket. But I did find something else—a tiny hole in one corner.

"What is it?" Terry asked.

I was almost afraid to answer. "Hold the coat," I said. And I bent down and looked at the inside of the coat.

The raincoat and the lining were sewed together! Oh, good, I thought. I started feeling along the seam. Then Terry guessed. He started feeling, too.

All at once, I felt a small bump.

There was a little hole in the seam. I poked my finger up inside. "Tear it open more," Terry said. So I did. And there was the ring!

"It must have fallen off your finger in the pocket. Then it fell through the hole in your pocket. There's your missing property, Captain Sanders."

Terry looked happy—and a lot of other things besides. "Thanks," he said. "Thanks a lot, Detective Ross."

I had solved my first case. That night I wrote to Cousin Mary about it—and, of course, I wrote the letter in invisible ink!